Pigs Might Fly!

MUDPUDDLE FARM

michael morpurgo

Cover illustrations by Cecilia Johannson

Interior illustrations by Shoo Rayner

HarperCollins *Children's Books*

And Pigs Might Fly first published in Hardback by
A&C Black (Publishers) Limited 1983
First published in paperback by Collins, a division of HarperCollins, 1988

Jigger's Day Off first published in Hardback by
A&C Black (Publishers) Limited 1989
First published in paperback by Collins, a division of HarperCollins, 1990

This bind-up edition first published by HarperCollins *Children's Books* 2008

This edition produced for The Book People Ltd,
Hall Wood Avenue, Haydock, St Helens, WA11 9UL

HarperCollins *Children's Books* is a division of
HarperCollins*Publishers* Ltd
77-85 Fulham Palace Road, Hammersmith, London W6 8JB

The HarperCollins *Children's Books* website address is
www.harpercollinschildrensbooks.co.uk

1

ISBN 978-0-00-783528-7

Printed and bound in England by
Clays Ltd, St Ives plc

Contents

Chapter One

There was once a family of all sorts of animals that lived in the farmyard behind the tumble down barn on Mudpuddle Farm.

At first light every morning Frederick, the flame-feathered cockerel, lifted his eyes to the sun and crowed and crowed until the light came on in old Farmer Rafferty's bedroom window.

Ah sweet mystery of light, at last I've found you....

One by one the animals crept out into the dawn and stretched and yawned and scratched themselves. But no one ever spoke a word—not until after breakfast.

Old Farmer Rafferty put in his teeth, looked out of his bathroom window and shook his head.

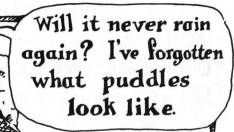

Will it never rain again? I've forgotten what puddles look like.

All my fields are burnt yellow and the stream's dried right up.

And he opened the window and shouted,

Go away, sun! You hear me? Run off and shine somewhere else. Go on, push off!

But the sun was too far away to hear. It just went on shining.

8

Chapter Two

Out in the farmyard the animals
looked up at the sun and sighed.

So they all put their hats on, except for Egbert the greedy goat who had already eaten his —

and Pintsize who thought pigs looked silly in hats. But then Pintsize *never* did what he was told.

Down at the pond Upside and
Down, the two white ducks that no
one could tell apart, had their heads
stuck in the mud because there was
hardly any water left in the pond.

Albertine sat still as a statue on her
island, shading her goslings under
her great white wings.

'When's it going to rain, Mum?'
they peeped.

'Sometime,' she said, and she
settled down to sleep because it was
the wisest thing to do and Albertine
was the wisest goose that ever lived
(and everyone knew it, including
Albertine).

So, thirsty and dusty and itchy, the animals trooped down to ask her advice, all except Mossop, the cat with the one and single eye, who was fast asleep on his tractor seat.

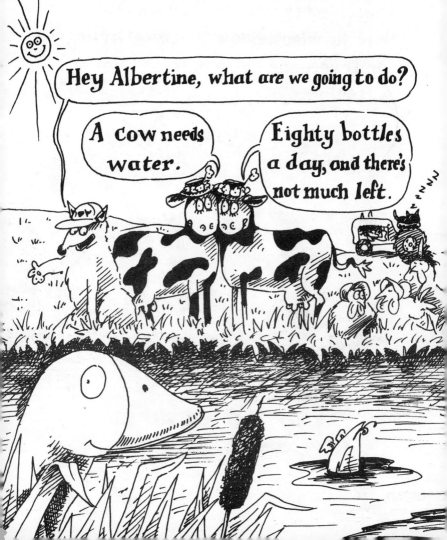

15

said Diana the
silly sheep.

'What about you?' said Jigger, the
almost-always sensible sheepdog.

Frederick looked up at the buzzards
and larks and swifts and swallows.
'If only I could fly like them. Must
be cool up there,' he sighed.

And little Pintsize looked up too
and thought just the same thing.

'You've got wings,' said Egbert.
'Use them.'

'Now, now,' said Captain. 'We're
quarrelling again.' And he called
out to Albertine.

So that's what they all did –
Captain in the darkest corner of his
stable,

Jigger under the
rhubarb leaves in
the vegetable patch,

Aunty Grace and Primrose side by
side under the great ash tree,

20

Egbert behind a pile of paper sacks
in the barn so he could be near his
lunch,

and Diana right in
the middle of the
sunniest field
because she was
very very silly!

Frederick went wherever his
speckled hens did – and as they all
went in different directions, he
found that very difficult!

While Peggoty and her little pigs, including Pintsize, crawled into a patch of nettles and lay still. Soon all the animals were fast asleep . . .

except Pintsize who wasn't at all sleepy.

Chapter Three

Of all Peggoty's little pigs Pintsize was definitely the naughtiest. Say 'do this' and he'd do that. Say 'come here', and he'd go there. It was just the way he was. Some children are like that.

He waited until Peggoty was snoring,

then tiptrottered through the farmyard

and down the lane

looking for really interesting things to do.

He hadn't gone far when he saw old Farmer Rafferty leaning on a gatepost and talking to the next-door farmer. Both of them were gazing up at the sky.

Farmer Rafferty shook his head as he squinted at the sun.

he said,
and he laughed like a drain.

Pintsize pricked up his ears, (which isn't easy for a little pig).

And he jumped up and down in wild excitement.

Chapter Four

Flying was not nearly as easy as it looked. Pintsize stood up on his back trotters and flapped his front ones – trotters, he thought, would do just as well as wings.

But however hard he flapped (and flapping trotters is *not* easy) and however much he jumped up and down, he somehow never managed to take off. But Pintsize was not a giving-up sort of pig. He sat down and thought about it.

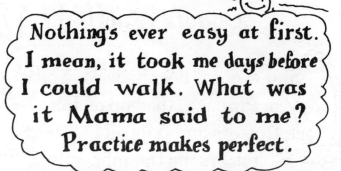

He was out in the
meadow, practising
his trotter flapping,
when a crow spotted
him and landed
beside him.

The crow cackled and flew off to tell his friends, then they all cawed together until they got sore throats – which served them right.

Suddenly Pintsize had an idea.

Upside and Down, they can fly. I've seen them. They'll teach me.

And he trotted off down to the muddy pond. 'Upside! Down!' he squealed, but they couldn't hear him, not with their heads in the mud.

UPSIDE! DOWN!

Shhh! Hush! Sorry! Quiet

BLUB   GLUG

In the end he got a long stick and poked
Upside
in his
down,

and Down
somewhere
else!

They were not at all pleased.

What do you want?

I want to fly.

'What, like this?' they quacked.
And they took off and looped a loop.

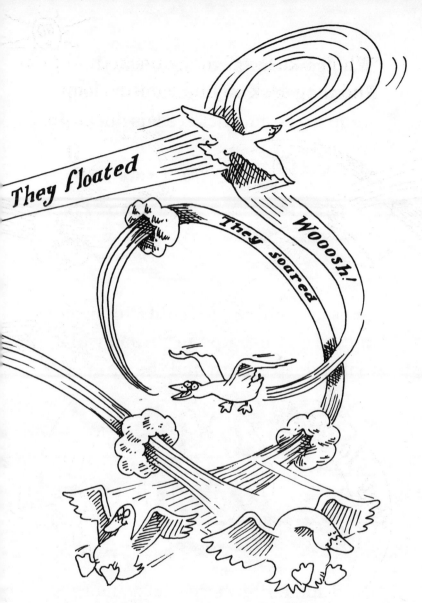

They floated

Wooosh!

They soared

They landed quite puffed. 'Like that?' they quacked.

'Yes,' said Pintsize. 'Just like that.
Please teach me. *Please.*' But they
sniggered and snickered as ducks do.

'Just you watch me,' said Pintsize,
and he climbed up the garden wall,
took a deep breath and then ran . . .

until suddenly there was no more
wall to run on . . . and he was flying
through the air!

For one wonderful moment he was up there with the birds, but then something was pulling him down and down and down and he was turning over and over . . . .

Then he landed,  in the muddy pond.

'Oh dear,' thought Albertine. 'I suppose I'd better do something about this.'

So she stood up and honked and honked until all the animals woke up and came running.

Pintsize was climbing the ladder
(and that's not easy if you're a pig)
up onto the haystack.

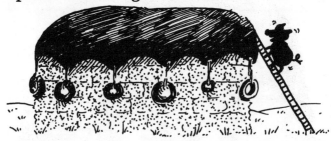

Peggoty closed her eyes, 'I'm not
looking,' she said.

We mustn't let him out of our
sight, otherwise he'll hurt
himself. Wherever he jumps
he's got to have a soft
landing. Quick Jigger,
you're the fastest.

Yap!

Yap!

W WOO

Yap!

Yap

That's my Mum,
making the hard
decisions.

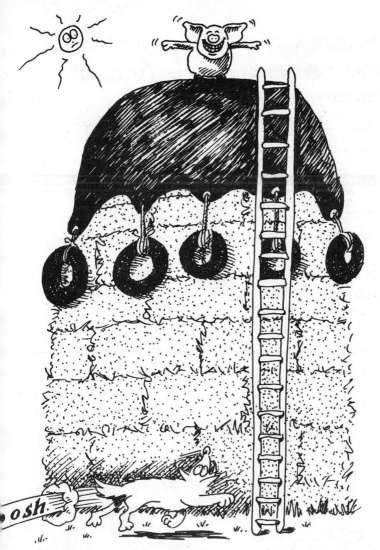

Jigger sprinted across the farmyard
until he was standing right under
the haystack. 'Don't jump!' he barked.
'Don't do it' . . . But Pintsize did it.

39

For one wonderful
moment he was
up there with the
birds, but then
something was
pulling him down
and down and
he was turning
over and over,
and then he landed –

SQUOOOOOF!

on Jigger's back.

Jigger never knew
that little pigs
could be that heavy.
But he knew now.

And very soon they all knew,
because wherever Pintsize went
they had to go, so that whenever he
jumped, one of them was always
there for him to land on.

Every time he jumped he flew
further – or he thought he did, 'I can
fly,' he'd squeal. 'Pigs can fly.'

And it was true – well, sort of.

Pintsize flew as far as a pig ever had flown, but then he'd drop like a stone and knock all the air out of poor Aunty Grace (and that's a lot of air),

or Primrose

or Captain

or Egbert

or Frederick.

But the one he liked landing on most was Diana, because she was very soft and very springy and very spongy.

'Thanks, Diana,' he'd squeak and off he'd go again before anyone could catch him.

This can't go on.
You can say that again.
This can't go on.

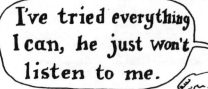

I've tried everything I can, he just won't listen to me.

Something's got to be done.

Too true, quite right.

But What?

Everyone looked at Albertine to see if she'd had one of her ideas.
And of course she had.

43

'Don't you worry,' she said. 'I'll have a word with a friend of mine. I've got friends in high places you know. Just you keep your eye on Pintsize, all of you.'

Chapter Five

Drooping in the heat of the day, the animals did as Albertine said and trailed around the farm after Pintsize. They found him teaching his brothers and sisters. Standing up on his back trotters, Pintsize was explaining how a pig flies.

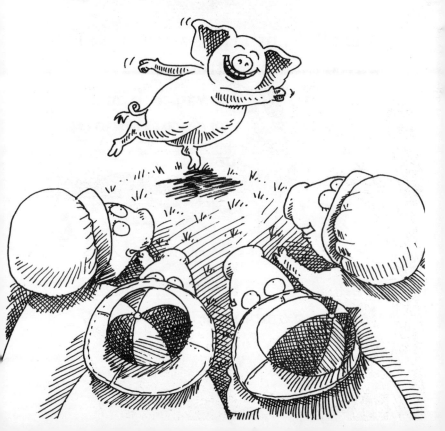

'You just wave these,' he said,
flapping his front trotters, 'and you
lift off. Simple when you know how.'

And all the little pigs stood up and
waved their front trotters.

I'd watch him if I were you, Peggoty.

But I can't look!

While she wasn't looking, a buzzard
flew down and landed beside
Pintsize.

'Am I ready?' said Pintsize. 'Course I'm ready!' And before he knew it, the buzzard had picked him up and was soaring into the sky high above the farm.

'Nice view,' said the buzzard.

Pintsize looked down, and wished he hadn't. His stomach started to turn over and he began to feel very sick and very frightened. The animals below him were getting smaller

and smaller.

Then he couldn't see them any more.

51

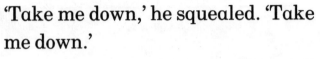
'Take me down,' he squealed. 'Take
me down.'

Pintsize tried to scream, but he couldn't. He was so frightened he couldn't even breathe . . .

53

The farm was coming closer and closer, it was getting bigger and bigger! He was going to crash!

Pintsize closed his eyes.

'Not yet,' said the buzzard, and as
they floated through the silent sky
they came to a cloud, a dark cloud.
'Don't like the look of that,' said the
buzzard a bit louder than he should.

Thunder rolled around the sky and the rain began to fall in great dollops.

'I want to go home,' squealed Pintsize. 'I want my mama.'

'All right,' said the buzzard, 'I'll drop you off.'

And he did just that!

Down below, Farmer Rafferty was talking to the next-door farmer again.

'Yippee! Yarroo!' cried old Farmer
Rafferty, and he did a sploshy rain-
dance in a muddy puddle. But if he
hadn't been so busy dancing, he'd
have noticed that it wasn't raining
cats and dogs at all – it was raining
pigs. And one little pig in
particular!

intsize tumbled through the air until at last he landed right in the middle of the....

DUNG HEAP

'Yes, Mama,' said Pintsize – and he
meant it. He snuggled into her and
buried his head in the dung so he
couldn't hear the thunder.

That evening Jigger saw Albertine
as she was having her bath.

'Maybe,' said Albertine and smiled
her goosey smile.

Meanwhile.......

On his tractor seat, Mossop
woke up.

Peggoty put her trotters over
Pintsize's ears so he couldn't hear
any more.

'If you insist,' sulked Mossop and he
yawned hugely as cats do, closed his
one and single eye and slept.

The night came down, the moon came up and everyone slept on Mudpuddle farm.

Chapter One

There was once a family of all sorts
of animals that lived in the farmyard
behind the tumbledown barn
down on Mudpuddle Farm.

Cocka-doodle-dooooo

At first light every
morning, Frederick
the flame-feathered
cockerel lifted his eye
to the sun and crowed
and crowed . . .

until the light
came on in old
Farmer Rafferty's
bedroom window.

One by one the animals crept out
into the dawn and stretched and
yawned and scratched themselves;
but no one ever spoke a word, not
until after breakfast.

'Jigger my dear,' said old Farmer Rafferty, one hazy hot morning in September.

Corn's as high as a house. Fair weather ahead, they say. Time has come for harvest, Jigger. So I shan't be needing you all day. It's your day off my dear. Old Thunder sleeps in his shed all year - now it's his turn to do some work. Got to earn his keep, just like all of us. I'll just go and rub him down.

And off he went.

'One day off a year,' thought Jigger, the always sensible sheepdog. 'One day a year when I don't have to be sensible, when I can do what a dog likes to do.' And he licked his smiling lips, and wagged his dusty tail.

71

Old Thunder lived all by himself in a shed at the end of the yard. No one ever went near him because no one dared.

Pintsize had never seen Old
Thunder. He longed to peek in
through the crack in the doors.

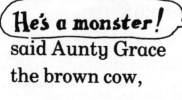

He's a monster!
said Aunty Grace
the brown cow,

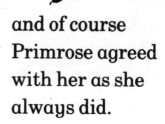

I agree.

and of course
Primrose agreed
with her as she
always did.

Matter of fact, most of the animals
thought Old Thunder was some sort
of monster.

So when old Farmer Rafferty opened the door of the shed that morning, all the animals went into hiding. Upside and Down turned upside down in terror. Mossop disappeared into a drainpipe. (Everyone was terrified of Old Thunder – except Egbert the greedy goat. He was always too hungry to be frightened.)

Albertine the white goose gathered her goslings around her on her island in the pond and explained everything to them. She wasn't just an intelligent goose, she was a wise mother as well.

At that very and same moment, there was a roar from inside Old Thunder's shed, and he rumbled out into the yard belching smoke and dust. Old Farmer Rafferty sat high and happy on the driver's seat singing his heart out.

'See, children,' said Albertine gently. 'I told you that's all Old Thunder is, just an old combine harvester.'

Chapter Two

Old Thunder sailed majestically out through the gate and into the corn field beyond, his great cutters turning like the wheels of a giant paddle steamer. 'One man went to mow, went to mow a meadow,' sang old Farmer Rafferty in his crusty, croaky kind of voice.

to mow, went to mow a meadow,

went to mow a m

And behind him, Jigger, the usually sensible sheepdog, slunk through the gate and lay down in the cut corn, his nose on the ground in between his paws.

SNIFF

He smelt something,

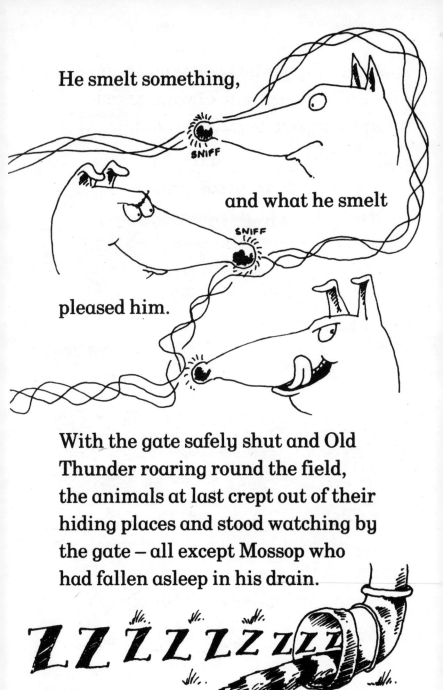

and what he smelt

pleased him.

With the gate safely shut and Old
Thunder roaring round the field,
the animals at last crept out of their
hiding places and stood watching by
the gate – all except Mossop who
had fallen asleep in his drain.

ZZZZZZZ

'What's Jigger up to?' asked Diana the silly sheep, who always asked questions but never knew any answers.

Round and round the field went old
Thunder, churning out the straw
behind him in long and golden rows.
Round and round the field went
Jigger, slinking low to the ground.

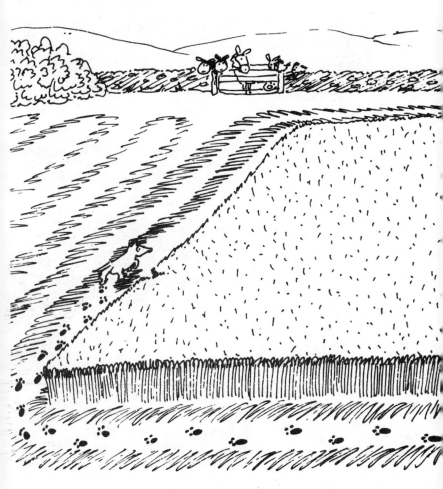

And every now and then he would
stop and stare at the square of
standing corn, and every time
he stopped, the square was a little
bit smaller.

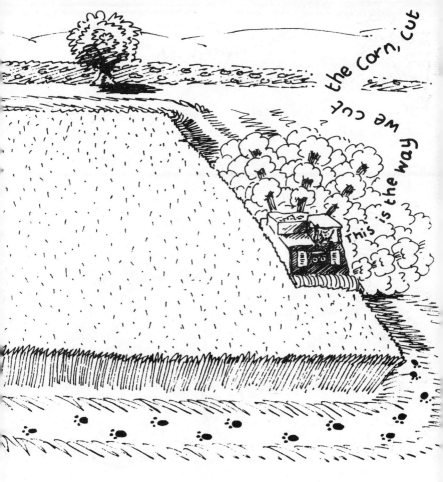

the corn, cut the cor

we cut

This is the way

'We shouldn't be standing around in the sunshine,' said Captain.

Best go inside, those flies'll be at us soon.

So they did.
Except for
Egbert
the goat
who was busy
chewing off
the paint
from the
iron-barred
gate.

At eleven o'clock Old Thunder

stopped, | shuddered, | coughed

and was silent. The birds sang
once more in the hedgerows.

Ever so carefully,
for he was stiff
in his knees,
old Farmer Rafferty
climbed down from
his seat and
sat down to rest
in the shade.

It was time for his morning milk. He *always* had it at eleven o'clock no matter where, no matter what.

'I'm making sure old Thunder doesn't miss anything,' said Jigger, but he never took his eyes off the standing corn.

And old Farmer Rafferty laughed because he knew better.

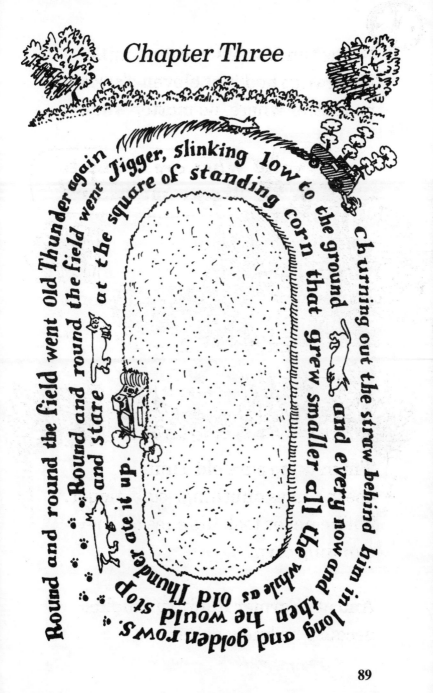

Round and round the field went Old Thunder again churning out the straw behind him in long and golden rows. Round and round the field went Jigger, slinking low to the ground and every now and then he would stop and stare at the square of standing corn that grew smaller all the while as Old Thunder ate it up.

Albertine was passing the gate with her three yellow goslings peeping behind her. 'What's Jigger up to?' they peeped.

'Never you mind,' said Albertine, hurrying them on. 'Jigger's not himself today, he never is on his day off. This is the one day of the year he's not sensible, and I don't want you to watch.'

I think he's Jiggered.

'Only mad dogs go out in the mid-day sun,' grumbled Egbert the goat, who had finished eating the paint on the gate.

'Mad dogs and goats,' said Albertine, but quietly so that Egbert would not hear. She never liked to upset anyone.

At one o'clock old Thunder stopped again, shuddered, coughed and was silent. The birds sang once more in the hedgerows.

Ever so carefully, old Farmer Rafferty climbed down from his seat and sat down to eat his lunch in the shade – pasties and pickles.

He offered some to Jigger for he knew Jigger was partial to pasties. But Jigger was not interested in pasties – not today – he had his eye on the golden square of standing corn.

No thanks, can't stop for lunch.

Round and round the field went
Old Thunder again

churning out the straw behind him

in long and golden rows.

Round and round the field

went Jigger, slinking low

to the ground.

Captain plodded slowly down to the pond for a drink. 'Egbert,' he said, 'is Jigger still out there in this heat?'

'Must be mad, that dog,' said Egbert. 'Hasn't stopped all day. Round and round and round he goes – makes you dizzy just to look at him. Dunno why he bothers – he never catches anything.'

At four o'clock Old Thunder stopped again, shuddered, coughed and was silent. The birds sang once more in the hedgerows. Ever so carefully old Farmer Rafferty climbed down from his seat and walked off back towards the farmhouse to fetch his tea.

'Not much more to do,' he said as he went. 'Got 'em well and truly bottled up, have you, my dear? You'll never get 'em, Jigger, you never do.'

But Jigger was not listening to old Farmer Rafferty. He lay with his chin on his paws, his ears pricked forward towards the corn, his nose twitching.

Rabbits and hares, his nose told him,
rats and mice, moles and voles,
pheasants and partridges, beetles
and bugs.

He could hear them all rustling and bustling and squeaking and squealing in the little golden square of standing corn that was left.

Sooner or later he knew they would have to make a run for it.

And he'd be waiting.

Chapter Four

> **Jigger my dear!**

It was old Farmer Rafferty calling from the house and whistling for him.

'Jigger! Come boy, come boy! I know it's your day off, but the sheep have broken out in Back Meadow. Come boy, come boy!'

> **I won't! It's my one day off. I'll be jiggered if I'll go!**

'Jigger! Jigger!' Old Farmer Rafferty
was using his nasty, raspy voice.

You come here
Jigger, else there'll
be trouble.

If I go now I'll
have wasted my
whole day. There'll
be nothing left
in that corn for
me to chase
when I get back.

And then he had an idea.

WOOF!
BARK!

Jigger's barking brought all the
animals running,

waddling

and flying
to the gate.

'Bring 'em all out into the field,
Captain,' he called out. The animals
all looked at each other nervously.

Don't worry
Old Thunder's
fast asleep.
He's been
working hard.

And so they all went out into the field, all except Diana the silly sheep who refused to go anywhere near old Thunder, whether he was asleep or not. Jigger quickly explained everything to Captain. And he went off towards the farmhouse.

In no time at all, Captain had them
all organised and ready.

So Peggoty and
her little pigs,

Including Pint size!

were sent to guard the north side of
the golden square of standing corn
along with Egbert.

I'd rather be
eating an old
shoe box

Primrose and Aunty Grace went off to guard the south side with Albertine and her goslings.

Captain himself stayed to guard the east side with Frederick the cockerel.

And Mossop, the cat with the one and single eye was sent off to guard the west side.

So on three sides of the golden
square of standing corn the animals
kept watch.

But for Mossop it was
all too much. The sun was hot

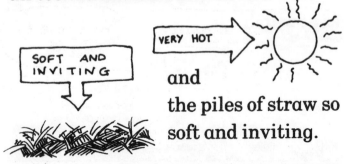

and
the piles of straw so
soft and inviting.

He lay down,

closed his one | and single eye | and

quite forgot what he was there for.

Chapter Five

Mossop snored as he slept, and
inside the golden square of corn
they heard him and saw him
and took their chance.

One by one the little creatures of the cornfield left their hiding places. In one long line they left – westwards . . .

Tee hee!

Rabbits first, then mice and

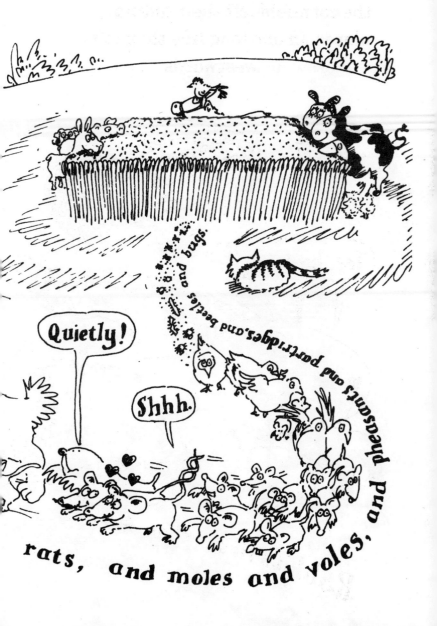

They tiptoed past the snoring cat
and out across the open field until
they reached the safety of the
hedgerow, where they vanished.

Chapter Six

Not long after this Jigger came
haring back through the gate.

Didn't let anything
escape, did you?

Not a one.
Proper job we
did for you Jigger,
proper job.

And all the animals hurried back to
the farmyard just in case Old
Thunder woke up again – all of
them except Mossop who still lay
fast asleep in a pile of straw.

'Just this last little square to finish, Jigger,' said old Farmer Rafferty after he had finished his tea. 'Be finished by sundown, in spite of those darned sheep.'

But Jigger was not listening. He
had other things on his mind. As Old
Thunder started up again he was
ready and waiting for the first of
the little creatures to break out of
their hiding place.

Round and round the field went Old Thunder for the last time, slinking low to the ground.

Round and round the field went Jigger for the last time,

and Round the Field

time churning out straw behind him in long and golden rows. Round

By the time the sun set behind the tumble-down barn, not a stalk of corn was left standing. And nothing had come out, no rabbit, no rat, no mouse, no vole, no mole, no pheasant, no partridge, no beetle and no bug.

Nothing.

'Well I'll be jiggered,' said Jigger.

'It's the sun, Jigger,' said Mossop, who had just woken up. 'Does strange things to you.'

Too much
sun and you
can see
things that
aren't there,

So I suppose
you can hear
things and
they're not
there.

I suppose
you can even
smell things
when they're
not there.

I can tell you Jigger nothing came past me when I was on guard. Well they wouldn't dare, would they?

And he yawned hugely as cats do.

Jigger looked at Mossop sideways and wondered.

'Had a good day off, Jigger my dear?' old Farmer Rafferty shouted as he passed by high up on Old Thunder.

And old Farmer Rafferty laughed
and laughed, until the laughter
turned into a song once again.

One man went to mow, went to mow a mea...

One man and his dog, (woof! woof!) went to m
It's been a long day. Don't know about you, Jigger, but I'm just about ready for bed.
Tee hee!

And the night came down and the moon came up and everyone slept on Mudpuddle Farm.